Badger's Race

Alison Catley

RED FOX

Badger's
Race

A Red Fox Book
Published by Random House Children's Books
20 Vauxhall Bridge Road, London SW1V 2SA
A division of The Random House Group Ltd
London Melbourne Sydney Auckland
Johannesburg and agencies throughout the world

Copyright text and illustrations © Alison Catley 1994

1 3 5 7 9 10 8 6 4 2

First published in Great Britain by Hutchinson Children's Books 1994
Red Fox edition 1999

Printed in Singapore

RANDOM HOUSE UK Limited Reg. No. 954009

ISBN 0 09 187303 7

'I'm strong, I'm fast; I'm a jolly fine fellow,'
said Fox to Badger one morning.

Just then, Hare whizzed by on his
long, strong legs.

'Humph!' said Fox. 'I'm faster than him. I'm faster than a deer, faster than a dog. I'm certainly faster than a *badger*.'

'I'm sure you are,' sighed Badger, who was anxious to be going about her business.

'Well, I think we should have a race,' announced Fox. 'Just so I can prove what a fine fellow I am.'

And he bullied and cajoled and pestered Badger until she finally agreed to take part. The race was to be across the whole countryside and over the mountain to the river on the edge of the town.

Off charged Fox like a bullet from a gun, heedless of anything or anyone who stood in his path. Dormouse went flying – her nest and food store all spoilt.

'Oh, dear me,' said Badger when she arrived at the sorry scene. And although she knew she should really be on her way, she stopped to gather up the scattered fruit and nuts and help Dormouse rebuild her nest.

When everything was as it should be, the animals shared a fine supper. But Badger was so tired she very soon fell fast asleep.

In the morning, Badger awoke with a start. The race! She quickly said goodbye to her new friends and hurried off. On she went across rivers and through forests; through rain and through mist.

All the time the weather was growing colder; it was hard
going and lonely, for many fellow creatures had gone to
sleep for the winter.

So Badger was glad when, one morning, she came across Hare foraging in a field all silver with frost.

'Have you seen Fox?' asked Badger. 'We're in a race.'

'Oh, him!' replied Hare. 'He charged through here yesterday, knocked me clean off my hind legs, and never even stopped to see if I was hurt!' And Hare looked so downcast that Badger sat and chatted with him for a while until his spirits lifted.

As evening came the first snowflakes of winter began to fall.

'Best be on my way,' said Badger.

Badger hadn't gone far when the snow began to fall more thickly. The wind picked it up and tossed it around in a blizzard and very soon Badger could hardly see the way ahead. She was just about to give up and turn for home when a shrill voice came to her on the wind.

'Over here, Badger,' it said.

Then out of the snow appeared
a stoat, all wintry white in his
ermine coat.

'I'm afraid I'm lost,' said Badger.
'I'm in a race with Fox, but this
blizzard has slowed me down.'

'Well, why don't you rest up here for a while?' said Stoat.

So Badger and Stoat sheltered together through the worst of the weather; they spent the evenings telling each other stories and by the time the snow had thawed they were the best of friends.

But when the first new buds of spring appeared in the earth, Badger said it was time she was on her way. She knew she had little chance of catching Fox, but a race once started must be finished.

Badger set off at a good pace, strengthened after her long rest. But all around, the countryside was bursting into new life – and she found herself stopping now and again to sniff at a flower or roll in the thick new grass. At the bottom of the mountain Badger met Duck, who begged her to come and see her new family of chicks. By the time Badger set off again, it was already afternoon.

At last, Badger began to climb the mountain. Up and up she went. She reached the top just as the sun set in a blaze of red and gold. Down below, she could see the river and the bridge that was to serve as a finishing post. She knew now that Fox must have won, but for all that, she was glad that she had stayed the course.

As Badger hurried down the mountain, she was startled by a frightened cry. She slipped and went hurtling down, landing with a bump on a rocky ledge. There, cowering with fright, was a tiny lamb who had fallen through a hole in the fence. Badger sighed. She was now very close to the finishing post but there was nothing for it. She took the little lamb on her back and carried it up the mountain to its mother.

Badger was exhausted. 'I'm in a race with Fox,' she told Sheep. 'I've been through rivers and through forests, through rain and through snow, and up and down this mountain. I don't think I can go on. And in any case, Fox has surely won.'

'Don't give up,' urged Sheep. 'Not now you are so close.' She called the flock together. 'We'll all come with you,' she said, 'and guide you safely down the mountain.'

As the party reached the finishing post, Fox
suddenly leapt out from the bushes.

'I won!' he cried. 'I've been here for weeks. Poor old Badger. I won! I won!'

Badger sighed. She thought about all her new friends, about the beauty of the first snowfall, the gentle colours of spring and the glorious sunset. 'Perhaps,' she said and she ambled off to enjoy the fine spring day.

Some
bestselling Red Fox
picture books

THE BIG ALFIE AND ANNIE ROSE STORYBOOK

by Shirley Hughes

OLD BEAR

by Jane Hissey

OI! GET OFF OUR TRAIN

by John Burningham

DON'T DO THAT!

by Tony Ross

NOT NOW, BERNARD

by David McKee

ALL JOIN IN

by Quentin Blake

THE WHALES' SONG

by Gary Blythe and Dyan Sheldon

JESUS' CHRISTMAS PARTY

by Nicholas Allan

THE PATCHWORK CAT

by Nicola Bayley and William Mayne

WILLY AND HUGH

by Anthony Browne

THE WINTER HEDGEHOG

by Ann and Reg Cartwright

A DARK, DARK TALE

by Ruth Brown

HARRY, THE DIRTY DOG

by Gene Zion and Margaret Bloy Graham

DR XARGLE'S BOOK OF EARTHLETS

by Jeanne Willis and Tony Ross

WHERE'S THE BABY

by Pat Hutchins